British Library Cataloguing in Publication Data

A catalogue record for this book is available from the British Library

ISBN 0 340 56264 1

This compilation copyright © Thelma Simpson 1992
Illustrations copyright © Tessa Hamilton/Simon Girling Associates 1992

This compilation first published 1992

Published by Hodder and Stoughton Children's Books,
a division of Hodder and Stoughton Ltd,
Mill Road, Dunton Green, Sevenoaks, Kent TN13 2YA

Designed by Trevor Spooner
Photoset by Litho Link Ltd, Welshpool, Powys, Wales
Printed in Hong Kong

The
Ten-Minute
BEDTIME STORYBOOK

HODDER AND STOUGHTON
LONDON SYDNEY AUCKLAND

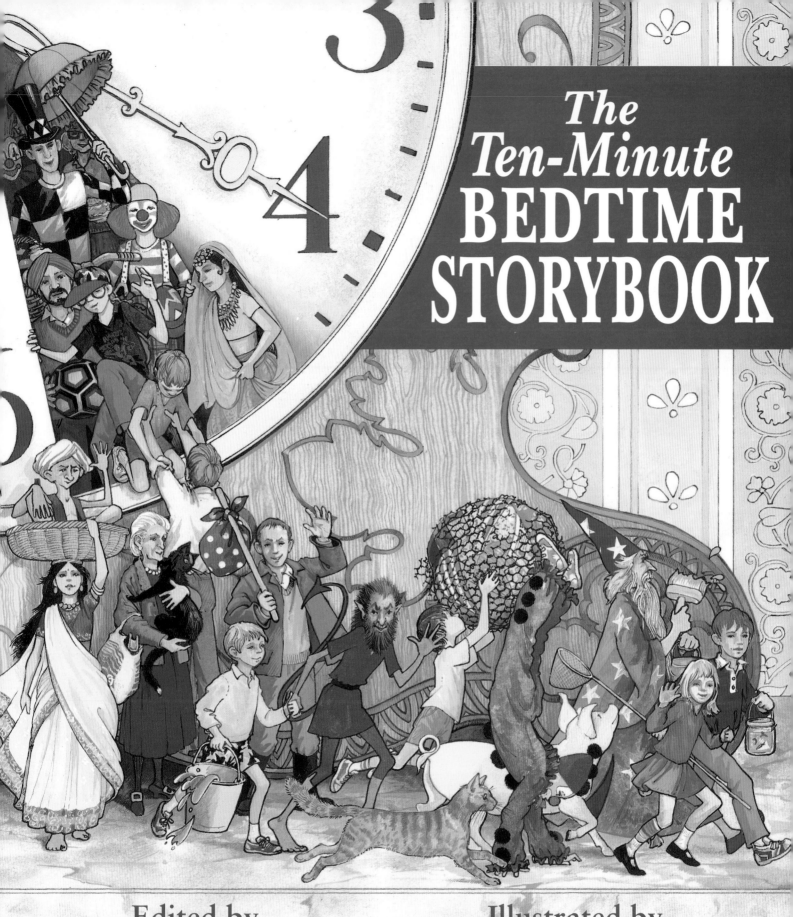

The *Ten-Minute* BEDTIME STORYBOOK

Edited by
THELMA
SIMPSON

Illustrated by
TESSA
HAMILTON

For Mike, Claire and Philip

The editor, Thelma Simpson, is grateful to those families in the Federation of Children's Book Groups who gave this collection their seal of approval. A proportion of the royalties from the sale of this book will go to help this charity.

Acknowledgments

The editor and publishers are grateful to the following for permission to reproduce the stories in this collection:

The Arguing Boy © Leila Berg 1983 (from *Tales for Telling*), Methuen Children's Books; *The Boy Who Made Things Up* © Margaret Mahy 1982 (from *The Chewing Gum Rescue and Other Stories*), J.M. Dent & Sons; *The Great Blueness and Other Predicaments* © Arnold Lobel 1968, World's Work Ltd/William Heinemann Ltd; *Irritating Irma* © Robin Klein 1980 (from *Runaway Shoes and Other Stories*), reprinted by permission of Curtis Brown Ltd; *Jason's Rainbow* © Joan Aiken 1986 (from *Never Meddle with Magic and Other Stories*), reprinted by permission of the author; *The Magic Lake* © Rani Singh 1984 (from *Indian Storybook*), William Heinemann Ltd; *The Outside Cat* © Jane Thayer 1957, reprinted by permission of the author; *Tall Inside* © Jean Richardson 1988, Methuen Children's Books; *Tilly Witch in the Park* © Pat Kremer 1983 (from *Mists and Magic* [ed. D. Edwards]), Lutterworth Press; *The Tooth-Ball* © Philippa Pearce 1987, André Deutsch Ltd.

CONTENTS

THE BOY WHO MADE THINGS UP

by Margaret Mahy

There was once a father who had a little boy. However, it was a bit of a waste for this father to have a boy, really, because he was much too interested in work. He worked all the week and then, at the weekends, he spent all his time under the car fixing it so that he would be able to go to work again the next week. You will understand he did not have much time to spend with his little boy. In fact, all the little boy ever saw of his father was a pair of boots sticking out from under the car. This was not much fun. With no father to tell him exciting stories, the boy had to make up his own stories. He became very good at making things up.

Well, one day the father's car broke down a long way from home and had to be taken away to a garage, and there was not much for the father to do at the weekend. He felt bare and unprotected with no car to crawl under. The space of hills and sky made him feel nervous. However, he decided to make the best of it all, and take his boy for a walk instead.

'Come on, Michael,' he called. 'We'll wander down to the crossroads, shall we?'

Michael was delighted to go for a walk with his father. He marched cheerfully along beside him, looking at him curiously. He wasn't used to seeing all of his father at the same time. After a while he said, 'Shall we just walk along, Dad, or shall we make some of it up?'

'Make some of it up?' said the puzzled father. 'Make what up? . . . Oh well, whatever *you* like, Michael,' he added in a kind voice.

'Shall we go by *that* path then?' said the little boy, pointing. Over the field ran a path that the father did not recognise. It was narrow, and a bit tangled, with foxgloves leaning over it, and bright stones poking through the ground.

'That's funny!' said the father. 'I've never seen that path before. There's no doubt you miss a lot by driving everywhere. Where does this path go?'

'It goes to the sea,' said Michael, leading the way, brushing the dew off the foxgloves.

'But the sea is fifty kilometres away,' cried the father. 'It can't lead to the sea.'

'We're making it up, remember,' said Michael.

'Oh, just pretending,' the father replied, as if everything was understood and ordinary again.

'The sea is on the other side of that little hill,' Michael went on, and the father was amazed to see the path hump itself into a little hill in front of them. At the same time a soft murmuring filled the air, as if giants were breathing quietly in their sleep. The father and Michael hurried up the little hill. There on the other side was the sea. The sand stretched a long way, starred with shells, striped with seaweed. There was no one else on all that long sunny shore. There weren't even any seagulls – just the sand, with the sea dancing along its edge.

'I told you. I told you,' yelled Michael, and charged on to the beach. His father followed him, frowning with amazement.

'If I'd known we were coming here,' he said, trying hard to make his voice sound ordinary, 'I'd have brought buckets and spades.'

'There are buckets and spades over by that log,' Michael told him. 'And our togs! Mine are wrapped up in a blue towel. What about yours?'

'Er . . .' said his father.

'Just make it up,' Michael cried. 'I'll make it up for you. An orange towel, almost new.'

The log lay, half in, half out of the sand, as if it was trying to burrow down and get away from the sun. There were the buckets and spades. There were the togs and towels.

'Swim first!' decided Michael. 'It's a bit coldish. Let's make it a warm day.'

Immediately the wind died down and the sunshine grew hotter. The father stood frowning at his orange towel, almost new.

'I'm ready,' Michael said, dancing before him. 'You're slow, Dad. Last one in is nothing but a sand flea.' He sped, running and jumping, into the waves. The sand-flea father followed.

'Be careful!' he shouted. 'Remember you can't swim, and I haven't done much swimming myself for a few years.'

'Say you're a wonderful swimmer!' suggested Michael. 'Say we can both swim to the islands.'

'The islands?' said the father. Sure enough, out on the horizon were islands scattered like seeds in the furrows of the sea.

The boy and his father swam out to the islands without getting in the least bit tired. The water was warm, yet tingling, and as clear as green grass. Shoals of bright fish, as small and shiny as needles, followed them and tickled their feet. Down, down, far down under the water, the sand shone silver with black fish all over it, like a night sky pulled inside out. The boy and his father swam in and out among the islands. Waves burst on the rocks around them and rainbows in the spray curled over their heads. Sometimes they swam on their fronts, peering down through the clear water, watching fish and sand.

'I could swim all day,' the father cried.

'But we've got to get back for our ice-creams,' declared Michael.

So they swam lazily back to the long, empty beach, still quiet except for the sighing, breathing sea.

'Here! Where will we get any ice-creams?' asked the father, frowning again. 'There are no shops.'

'Can't you understand how things work yet?' Michael cried despairingly. 'We make something up! Look!'

Far down the beach something was moving closer and closer. It was a tall thin man dressed in black and white squares, like a harlequin or a chess board. He was holding a blue frilly sunshade over his head with one hand and carrying a basket in the other. With his feet he furiously peddled a yellow bicycle. As he passed them he put the basket into Michael's hands. Then he turned his bicycle and rode straight into the sea. For a few minutes his blue sunshade bobbed above the water and then a green wave curled slowly over it, like a curtain coming down at a theatre. They couldn't see him any more.

'See what I mean?' asked Michael. 'Much better than a shop.'

The basket was full of ice-cream with nuts in it, and strawberries on top. The father looked very grown-up and thoughtful. After they had eaten the ice-cream, they played with their buckets and spades for a while, and then they decided it was time to go back down the foxglove path. All the way home the father looked more and more thoughtful and grown-up. Everytime he looked at Michael he blinked.

As soon as they got home, Michael was sent to wash his hands – a thing that usually happens to boys. The father stood beside the mother, drying up the dishes she was washing.

'Tell me, my dear,' he said, in a quiet, nervous voice. 'Does Michael often make things up?'

'Oh yes!' said his mother. 'He's rather a lonely little boy and he's always making up some adventure. He's very good at it.'

'But,' said his father in a very astonished voice, 'he took me to the *beach*. We went *swimming*. I got *sunburned*. My shoes are full of *sand*. And yet I *know* the sea is fifty kilometres away.'

'Oh yes,' said the mother very casually, 'I told you. He's very good at making things up. I've told you before, but you were too busy listening to the car.'

'It's very strange – very strange,' said the father.

'But lots of fun!' the mother added.

'Yes, I suppose it is,' said the father. He thought some more.

'I don't think I'll spend so much time with the car from now on. Michael needs the guidance of a father. A father and son should see a lot of each other, don't you think?' he asked.

'Oh yes, I'm sure they should,' said the mother, and she smiled a smile that was almost a grin at the saucer she was washing.

THE GREAT BLUENESS
AND OTHER PREDICAMENTS
by Arnold Lobel

*L*ong ago there were no colours in the world at all.
Almost everything was grey, and what was not grey
was black or white.

It was a time that was called The Great Greyness.

Every morning a Wizard who lived during the time of
The Great Greyness would open his window to look out
at the wide land.

'Something is very wrong with the world,' he would
say. 'It is hard to tell when the rainy days stop and the
sunny days begin.'

The Wizard would often go down the stairs to his dark,
grey cellar. There, just to amuse himself and to forget
about the drab world outside, he would make wonderful
magic potions and spells.

One day while the Wizard was mixing and stirring a
little of this and a bit of that, he saw something strange in
the bottom of his pot.

16

'What good looking stuff I have made!' he exclaimed. 'I will make some more right away.'

'What is it?' asked the neighbours, when they saw the Wizard painting his house.

'A colour,' said the Wizard. 'I call it *blue*.'

'Please,' cried the neighbours, 'please give us some!'

'Of course,' said the Wizard.

'And that was how The Great Blueness came to be. After a short time everything in the world was blue. Trees were blue. Bees were blue. Wheels and evening meals were blue. The Wizard would pedal out on his blue bicycle to look around at the wide, blue world. He would say, 'What a perfect day we are having.'

But The Blueness was not so perfect. After a long time all that blue made everyone sad. Children played no games. They sulked in their blue gardens. Mothers and fathers sat at home and stared gloomily at the blue pictures on the walls of their blue living rooms.

'This Blueness is too depressing,' said the neighbours to the Wizard, who was unhappier than anyone.

'Nobody laughs anymore,' he said. 'Even I myself have not smiled for days.'

'I must do something,' said the Wizard as he slouched down the stairs to his dark, blue cellar.

There he began to mix and stir a little of this and a bit of that. Soon he saw something new in the bottom of his pot. 'Now here is happier stuff,' said the Wizard. 'I will make some more right away.'

'What is that?' asked the neighbours when they saw the Wizard painting his fence.

'I am calling it *yellow*,' said the Wizard.

'May we have some?' begged the neighbours.

'You may,' replied the Wizard.

And that was how The Great Yellowness came to be.

After a short time everything in the world was yellow. There was not a flyspeck of blue anywhere to be seen. Pigs were yellow. Wigs were yellow. Stairs and dentist chairs were yellow.

17

The Wizard would gallop out on his yellow horse to explore the wide, yellow world. He would say, 'What a fine day we are having.'

But The Yellowness was not so fine. After a long time all that yellow began to hurt everyone's eyes. People walked about bumping and thumping into each other. They were squinting and could not see where they were going.

'This Yellowness is too bright and blinding,' said the neighbours to the Wizard.

'You don't have to tell me,' moaned the Wizard, who had a cold towel on his head. 'Everyone has a headache, and so do I.'

So the Wizard stumbled down the stairs to his dark, yellow cellar. There he mixed and stirred a little of this and a bit of that. Soon he saw something different in the bottom of his pot. 'This is handsome stuff,' declared the Wizard. 'I will make some more right away.'

'What do you call that?' asked the neighbours when they saw the Wizard painting his flowers.

'*Red,*' answered the Wizard.

'We would like some too,' pleaded the neighbours.

'Right away,' said the Wizard.

And that was how The Great Redness came to be. After a short time everything in the world was red. Mountains were red. Fountains were red. Limburger cheese and afternoon teas were red.

The Wizard would sail out in his red boat to see what he could see of the wide, red world. He would say, 'What a glorious day we are having.'

But The Redness was not so glorious. After a long time all that red put everyone into a very bad temper. Children spent their days fighting and punching each other while mothers and fathers argued loudly. A furious crowd of neighbours marched to the Wizard's house.

'This awful Redness is all your fault,' they shouted. Then they threw stones at the Wizard, who jumped up and down and gnashed his teeth because he was in such a terrible temper himself.

The Wizard stormed down the stairs into his dark, red cellar. He mixed and stirred for many days. He used all the magic that he could think of to find a new colour, but all that he made was more and more blue, more and more yellow, and more and more red. The Wizard worked until all of his pots were filled to the top.

The pots were so full that they soon overflowed. The blue and the yellow and the red all began to mix together. It was a terrible mess.

But when the Wizard saw what was happening, he exclaimed, 'That is the answer!' And he danced joyfully around the cellar.

The Wizard mixed the red with the blue and made a new colour.

The Wizard mixed the yellow with the blue and made a new colour.

The Wizard mixed the yellow with the red and made a new colour.

'Hurrah!' he shouted, and he mixed the red and the

blue and the yellow in all kinds of different ways.

'Look at all these beautiful things I have made!' said the Wizard when he was finished.

'What are they?' asked the neighbours.

'I call them purple and green and orange and brown,' said the Wizard.

'They are a sight for sore eyes,' cried the neighbours, 'but which one shall we choose this time?'

'You must take them all,' said the Wizard.

The people did take all the colours the Wizard had made. After a short time they found good places for each one. And after a long time when the Wizard opened his window, he would look out and say, 'What a perfectly fine and glorious day we are having!'

The neighbours brought the Wizard gifts of red apples and green leaves and yellow bananas and purple grapes and blue flowers.

At last the world was too beautiful ever to be changed again.

IRRITATING IRMA
by Robin Klein

I rma was very good at climbing. Her parents were calm people, who, if they saw Irma clamber up a church steeple or the outside of a lighthouse, would just murmur admiringly, 'Lovely, darling.' So when they took a holiday cottage near some steep cliffs and Irma told them she was going looking for eagles, they just said, 'Lovely, darling.'

Irma began to climb the cliffs and half-way up she found a little door. The door belonged to a dragon who was having a very nice long sleep, and he wasn't a bit pleased to be woken up. He stared at Irma's teeth braces and glasses and he wasn't very impressed. He rumbled like a forge.

'What a cute green lizard!' said Irma.

The dragon, insulted, uttered a huge echoey roar which splintered granite flakes from his cave.

'That's a nasty cough you've got,' said Irma.

The dragon eyed her Spiderman T-shirt and torn jeans and the cap that she had got free from a service station. He remembered clearly that maidens usually wore dear little gold crowns and embroidered slippers, and they

always squealed when they met him and looked ill at ease. He glared at Irma and spurted forth a long, smoky orange flame.

'No wonder you've got a cough,' said Irma. 'Smoking's a nasty habit and bad for your health. And this cave certainly is musty and it needs airing.'

The dragon made a noise like bacon rashers frying but Irma was busy inspecting everything. 'You need a broom for a start,' she said. 'And maybe a cuckoo clock up there by the door. Tch! Just look at the dust over everything! Tomorrow I'll bring some cleaning equipment and anything else I can think of.'

When she left, the dragon set to work, only he didn't do any dusting. He collected boulders and filled up the cave entrance. Bouldered up, and fortressed up, and buttressed up, he smiled grimly to himself and went back to sleep.

Some hours later he woke to a whirring headachy rumbling. Granite chips rattled around his ears, and Irma scrambled in, carrying a bright pneumatic power drill. 'Good morning,' she called. 'There must have been a landslide during the night. But I cleaned it up.'

The dragon's scales rattled. Angry little flames flickered in his jaw. He made a noise like a hundred barbecues and he squinted ferociously at Irma.

'Don't frown like that,' she ordered, tying on an apron. 'You'll end up with ugly worry lines. There's a lot of work to get through this morning. First I'll sweep this gritty sand away, and you could really do with a nice carpet in here, or maybe tiles would be better. If there's one thing I just can't stand, it's disorder.'

The dragon sizzled fretfully, but worse was to come. When Irma finished tidying up, she turned her attention to him. She bossily trimmed and lacquered his claws. She polished his scales and lifted up his wings and dusted under them with talcum powder. The dragon blushed but Irma didn't take any notice, because she was busy tying a blue ribbon around his tail. 'I've got to be going now,' she said. 'But I'll be back tomorrow.'

The dragon watched her climb down the cliff. 'There's only one way to get any peace,' he thought. 'I'll just have to eat her. Tomorrow. Freckles will taste nasty, and so will ginger hair, but maybe if I shut my eyes and gulp, it won't be so bad.' He groaned. Parents, he knew from past experience, usually came looking for devoured maidens, waving lances and acting very unfriendly.

When Irma arrived next morning, he opened his jaws, without much enthusiasm, ready to eat her, but Irma said, 'Look what I brought you!'

She shoved a plate under his nose. On it was a layer cake with strawberry cream filling, iced with chocolate icing and whipped cream, sprinkled with hundreds and thousands, lollies and meringues. The dragon shuddered weakly and felt ill.

'You look as though you're coming down with the flu,' said Irma. She took his temperature and spread a blanket over him. The blanket was fluffily pink and edged with satin binding, and the dragon thought it was very babyish. Irma wrapped it around him and fastened it with a kitten brooch. 'I'll leave you to get some rest now, you poor thing,' she said.

'You will?' thought the dragon hopefully.

'But I'll drop by first thing tomorrow,' said Irma. 'It's lucky for you I still have three weeks of my holiday left.'

And for three weeks, every day, she came, and the dragon suffered. She decorated his cave with pot plants and cushions, a beanbag chair, posters, a bookcase, calendars, and a dart board, and she brought along a toothbrush and bullied him into cleaning his teeth.

But at last, one morning, she said, 'I've got to go back to school tomorrow. You'll just have to look after yourself till next summer holidays.'

When Irma left, the dragon purred and capered about the cave. 'Hooray!' he thought. 'Good riddance! No more boring chatter and no more being organised, and best of all, undisturbed sleep!' He curled up and shut his eyes.

But his dreams were fretful, and he got up at daybreak feeling tetchy and cross. He paced his cave and wondered why the silence seemed weary, and the hours bleak and long. He brooded and nibbled at a claw, and crouched in his doorway staring down at the beach, but it was empty, because all the holiday people had gone. Irma had gone.

'Hooray!' he roared. 'And she won't be back for many glorious months!'

But why, he wondered glumly, were tears rolling down his cheeks?

Everywhere he looked in his cave he saw things Irma had lugged up the cliff to decorate his cave without permission. 'Yuk,' said the dragon morosely, and he kicked a pot plant over the cliff. A wave snatched at it, and the dragon gave a roar of anger and slithered down the cliff and grabbed it back. He carried it crossly back to his cave and plonked it down on Irma's bookcase.

'Even when she's not here, she's irritating,' he thought. 'I should have eaten her and got it over with. And the very next time I see her, irritating Irma will be my next meal! Freckles and all! Just wait!'

And he waited, but all his little flames flickered out one

24

by one, and his scales lost their sparkle, and his ribboned tail drooped listlessly. Winter howled through his cave, and he brooded, and led a horrid, bad-tempered life.

But at last gay umbrellas began to blossom like flowers along the beach, and it was summer. The dragon sharpened his teeth against the rocks and tried to work up an appetite. And the day came when Irma bounced in through his door, and the indignant dragon opened his massive jaws wide.

'Hello!' cried Irma. 'I meant to write, but I forgot your address, but just look what I brought you! Suntan lotion, and a yo-yo with a long string so it will reach down to the bottom of the cliff, and a kite with a picture of you on it, and now tell me, did you miss me? I certainly missed *you!*'

The dragon blinked in despair at her tangly plaits and glasses and teeth braces. 'She's talkative and tedious and her manners are terrible!' he reminded himself fiercely.

('And yet,' he thought, 'it's strange, but I rather like her face.')

'Nonsense!' he roared to himself. 'She's annoying and bossy and an utter little nuisance, and no one invited her here; she just walks in as though she owns the whole cliff!'

('And yet,' he thought, 'of all the maidens all forlorn, I rather like her best.')

'Didn't you miss me?' demanded Irma.

The dragon began to shake his head indignantly, but try as he could to prevent it, the headshake turned into a nod.

'Then we'll celebrate,' said Irma. 'What would you like for lunch?'

'Plain scones, please, Irma,' said the dragon.

THE MAGIC LAKE
by Rani Singh

In the kingdom of Rajasthan there once lived a rajah who had three daughters. The youngest, whose name was Purnima, was sweet-natured and obedient, but her sisters were jealous and scheming.

One day the oldest sister said, 'I am going to marry the richest man in the whole of India.'

The second sister said, 'I am going to marry the most handsome man in the whole of India.'

They both turned to Purnima and waited to hear what she would say.

'I will marry whoever my father chooses for me,' said Purnima.

'She's just saying that to please you, father,' the wicked sisters scoffed. 'She doesn't really mean it.'

'I do,' said Purnima. 'I will obey my father.'

So the sisters teased and tormented Purnima until their father intervened. 'I believe Purnima would marry whoever I chose for her, even if it were a ragged beggar,' he said.

26

'Then prove it!' cried the wicked sisters.

And so determined was the foolish rajah to prove how obedient his beloved daughter was that he said, 'Purnima, I command you to marry the first beggar you meet outside the city gates and to go away and live with him as your husband.'

So Princess Purnima was forced to leave the palace. As she went out of the city gates, there in front of her on the ground in a huge wicker basket, sat a small, ugly beggar. This was the man her father had commanded her to marry!

With a sigh, the princess looked at the miserable creature, whose head was misshapen and whose limbs were deformed.

'Hello,' she said to the beggar.

'Hello,' he squeaked back. He had a thin, strange voice and stared up at the princess with large, unblinking eyes. 'I can't walk. Will you carry me?'

Princess Purnima was gracious and kind, and felt sorry for this poor creature. She picked up the basket and placed it on her head. The load was heavy but he was her husband, and now she had no home she had no choice but to take him with her. Purnima walked out of the huge gates and away from the city. Carrying her husband in the basket on her head, the princess trudged from town to town. She worked and some days earned enough money to feed her husband and herself. She grew thinner and thinner. Her clothes became tattered and torn. But Purnima cared tenderly for her husband and even grew to love him.

One hot day, they came to a lake.

'It's so hot, princess,' squeaked the creature in the basket. 'Why don't you leave me here by the edge of this lake in the shade of the mango trees while you go off and find some food for us?'

'Very well,' said Purnima. 'I won't be long.'

Carefully she lowered the basket from her head, placed it under a tree by the water's edge, and set off to the nearby town.

Her husband sat in his basket and watched the birds and dragonflies round the lake. He saw an ugly black crow fly down to the water to drink and to bathe. It disappeared below the surface. The beggar waited for it to fly up again. Seconds passed, and the beggar's mouth dropped open in amazement, for the crow was nowhere to be seen. Instead, a white swan rose effortlessly out of the water. The ugly crow had changed into a beautiful swan!

The beggar could hardly believe his eyes. 'This must be a magic lake!' he said to himself. 'How could a crow change into a swan?' And if the lake had the power to change creatures, perhaps it could change him. Perhaps, if he too bathed in the clear water, he would become healthy and normal as he had once been. If only he could reach the water! He looked round desperately for help. There was not a soul to be seen. Even the swan had flown away. What could he do? He had to get to the lake!

He placed his arms on the sides of the basket and began rocking from side to side. Soon the basket was swaying violently. One more heave, the basket tumbled over and the beggar fell out on to the ground.

Slowly, painfully, he pushed himself the right way up. Using his elbows for support, he scrambled down to the edge of the lake. The water looked cool and inviting, but deep enough to drown in. The beggar crawled in. He immersed himself completely in the magic water, leaving only the tip of the little finger of his left hand untouched.

Then a wonderful thing happened. The beggar felt, and saw, his limbs become straightened. He felt life flowing into his legs. He was healthy, handsome and strong again, as he had once been. Joyfully, he strode out of the water and stood by the basket.

Just then the princess returned from the town, a bag of food in her hand. She looked at the basket. It was lying upturned where she had left it. There was no sign of the poor crippled beggar whom she had left behind. Instead, a handsome young man was standing, smiling, one hand on his hip, the other outstretched towards her.

The princess's eyes filled with tears. She thought this man must have killed her husband. 'Where is he?' she cried. 'What have you done with him?'

'I *am* your husband. He is not dead,' said the young man. 'You see, my sweet one, this lake where you left me to cool off is a magic lake. It has the power to change living creatures. So I decided to try my luck and managed to get myself down into the water. And look what happened!'

'How can you expect me to believe that?' said the princess. 'You must have killed my husband and now you're lying to me.'

'I knew you'd find my story hard to believe,' replied the prince (for so he was). 'So I deliberately left one part of my body out of the water when I bathed, to prove that my words were not false. Look.'

He held up his left hand and showed her the tip of his little finger. It was dark and misshapen, and the princess recognised it as belonging to the man she had married.

The prince walked to the edge of the lake and dipped his finger in the water. The princess watched in silence. As the prince held up his hand again, Purnima saw that the tip of his little finger was now smooth and strong, just like the rest of his hand and not crooked and ugly as it was before.

'Now do you believe me, Purnima?' said the prince.

He went on to explain that, many years earlier, an evil witch had placed a curse on him, and turned him from a prince into a poor deformed man, forced to beg for a living. But with the true love of a noble princess, and by bathing in the magic lake, the curse had been lifted and the prince restored to his normal shape.

'But through all these hard months, after being banished from your father's palace,' said the prince, 'and without knowing who I really was, Purnima, you have loved me and cared for me like a truly devoted wife. Come back with me now to my palace where you shall be crowned queen and I will surround you with all the love, comfort, happiness and wealth that you deserve. This is my promise to you, my Princess Purnima.'

The prince held out his arms and Purnima, overwhelmed with happiness, ran into them.

The prince did indeed keep his promise to his wife, and, as you can imagine, they lived happily ever after.

And to this day, the lake is said to have special healing properties, and is a place of pilgrimage for those who believe in miracles and fairy stories.

TALL INSIDE
by Jean Richardson

Joanne was small for her age. When they stood in line at school, she was the shortest person in her class.

'You'll catch up one of these days,' her mother said, as if it didn't matter.

'All the best things come in small packages,' her father said, giving her a kiss.

'You could try eating rubber bands. Then you might stretch,' her brother Matt said.

They just didn't understand.

Most days Jo went next door to play with her best friend Jenny. They had just learned how to do handstands and spent hours in the garden practising.

One day Jenny's cousins Rosie and Ann joined them.

'Let's start a club,' said Rosie, who couldn't do handstands. 'To join you have to pass a test. Everyone has to jump up and swing from that branch.'

Rosie did it easily, because she was tall. Jenny and Ann just made it. Jo couldn't reach at all.

'You can't join,' Rosie told her. 'You're too short.'

'I don't want to join your silly club anyway,' said Jo. And ran off home.

But she did. She went up to her bedroom and told her bear, Humpty. Tears splashed on to him, but he was used to getting wet.

'Anyone want to come shopping with me?' her father called up the stairs.

'Yes,' said Jo, quickly drying her eyes on Humpty.

On the way home they saw a ring of people laughing and clapping at something.

'What's going on?' Jo asked. 'Oh please, let's find out.'

Her father could see over the heads of the crowd, but Jo had to wriggle her way to the front.

The first thing Jo saw was a pair of striped trouser-legs that seemed to go right up into the sky. Miles up was a clown face with a cherry nose and a huge smile. He was the tallest man Jo had ever seen. A small man was trying to give the clown a message.

'Hey, Lofty!' he shouted, but Lofty didn't hear him. He waved his handkerchief, but Lofty didn't see him. Finally he began juggling with coloured balls. Lofty tried to catch them but he wasn't quick enough.

'Come and help me,' he called to the crowd. 'Who's good at catching things?'

'Me! Me!' several children shouted, and Lofty invited them to join him in the ring.

'Me! Me!' Jo shouted, but Lofty didn't see her. She was too small.

'Me! Me!' she shouted again, but her voice only reached to Lofty's waist.

He turned away, but Jo wouldn't give up. She ran after him and tugged at his trousers. The crowd laughed.

'What have we here?' Lofty said, peering down.

'Please can I help?' It was Jo's biggest voice, and it made her cheeks as red as Lofty's nose.

'Shall we let her help?' Lofty asked, and the crowd roared, 'Yes.'

The children followed Lofty to a van where they climbed in and found a pile of clown costumes. Jo wanted the red one with black pompoms, and pulled it away from another girl. A girl with spiky blue hair was in charge of makeup. She rubbed white greasepaint on Jo's face and ringed her eyes with black circles. Then she drew her a big upturned mouth.

One boy had a clown wig with hair sprouting from a bald patch. Jo wore a red nose like Lofty's. A clown showed them how to do somersaults on a big mat, and they all rolled over – and over. A boy did cartwheels and

Jo did her handstand – and stayed up for ages. The crowd clapped.

Then they paraded round the ring, copying the clown's funny walk. Jo waved to her father. Then she waved to Lofty, and he threw her a squeaker that made a rude noise.

When the show was over, Jo didn't want to take off her clown outfit. She shook her head when the makeup girl offered to clean her face.

The girl smiled. 'Do you want to keep the red nose?' she asked. Jo nodded. 'OK. It's yours.'

Jo looked at her spiky blue hair and thought she was the luckiest person in the world. Imagine being a clown every day!

Suddenly Lofty put his head round the door of the van. He was much too tall to climb inside. One minute he towered above Jo. The next he hopped into the van and was sitting beside her. Jo couldn't believe it. Then she saw a pair of legs in long striped trousers leaning against the side of the van. Lofty smiled. 'You didn't think my legs were that long, did you?'

'Well . . .' Jo didn't want to admit she had. 'It must be wonderful to be so tall,' she said. 'Especially when you're small like me.'

Lofty measured her with his eyes. 'When you've finished growing,' he said, 'I reckon you'll be looking down on me.'

'But don't you mind being short? I do.'

Lofty's eyes twinkled. 'The way I look at it,' he said, 'I don't mind being small because I can make people laugh. And that makes me feel tall inside.'

Over supper that night Jo and her father told her mother and Matt all about the clowns and about how good Jo had been. Matt was jealous. He wanted to try on the red nose, but Jo wouldn't take it off.

'You'll have to take your makeup off before you go to bed,' her mother said. 'You can't be a clown for ever, darling.' She gave Jo a cleanser and some tissues.

Jo looked at her clown face in the mirror for the last time. She felt she was saying goodbye to the clowns. First she wiped off her great big eyes. Then she wiped off her bright red cheeks. And finally she wiped off her great big mouth. But she took the red nose and put it under her pillow.

Wait till I tell Jenny, she thought. And she fell asleep, smiling.

TILLY WITCH IN THE PARK

by Pat Kremer

*T*illy Witch sat on a bench in the park eating a pink whippy ice-cream. Scuffle, her black cat, sat alongside, licking drips with a small, quick tongue. The sun shone brightly. Families lay quietly on the grass on rugs; children played, parents snoozed, young boys and girls chatted; it was very peaceful.

Tilly Witch sighed – she was bored. Witch business was not very good these days. Few people came to consult her in her neat little council flat. Very occasionally she was called upon to find lost dogs or rings. Sometimes she cured bad tummies or headaches. But these were dull spells – there had been very little chance to try out some interesting ones recently. Ingredients, too, were difficult to find. She knew where to search for spiders' webs and mouse whiskers – she crept round people's greenhouses and cellars, probing into the darkest and dustiest corners; and she searched church belfries to retrieve bats' wings (from ones that had already died, of course). But she had stopped collecting frog-spawn since reading that it had become very scarce, and she felt it was cruel to dig for wriggly, fat worms. Life was very difficult – modern times were no good for real old-fashioned witches.

Glumly, she reached for her Spell Book, which she always carried in her plastic bag.

"Newts . . . breasts of robins . . . legs of toads . . . wings of butterflies . . . tongues of mice . . .'

Tilly Witch shuddered. She read on. Her fingers rested at Chapter 215. She smiled – this looked better: 'How to Restore Lost Youth.' Next to it was another good one, 'How to create a Sea-Monster.'

Interesting and, looking at the ingredients, possible. Perhaps – here and now – why not?

She crouched behind some shrubs and whispered to the cat.

Scuffle ran around collecting rose petals and crab apples, empty snail-shells and a soft bird's feather, gleaming red berries and emerald pond slime, frothy spider's spit and sharp holly prickles. Tilly Witch flung them into an empty plant pot and began to stir them with a stick. She added three drops of rain water from a puddle and ten drops of dew from a shiny, cupped leaf growing in the darkest, coolest corner of the park.

'Six centipede's legs, six centipede's legs,' she muttered. But when Scuffle dropped the wriggly, tickly insect into her hand she looked at it for a while and then replaced it under a damp log.

'We'll just have to try to make it work without,' she said, and began softly to sing the spells: the Earth Spirits' Spell first, and then the Water Spirits'.

The softest of grey mists rose from the plant pot.

A small boy was watching her curiously, fishing-net in hand. 'You're a witch, aren't you?'

But before Tilly Witch had time to reply, his big sister

pulled him away: 'Don't be rude, Tom. There aren't any witches nowadays.'

Scuffle dipped her tail into the plant pot and swished it around, three times. Then she ran up the tallest tree, whose great branches stretched wide across the park and she flashed in and out among the leaves. Round and round whirled her tail and a cascade of rainbow-tinted droplets spun through the air on to the grass.

Mr Bannerjee, who had left his dress shop for the afternoon to bring his mother, wife and baby to the park, put out his hand, palm upward, and glanced at the blue sky twinkling through the leaves.

'That's strange. It feels like rain,' he said.

He had been very busy in the shop selling clothes and putting away new stock. He had been feeling quite old and tired.

Some children ran up with a ball – Joshua, Helen and Derek. Mr Bannerjee flicked out his foot very quickly, the ball rose high in the air and seemed to loop the loop before it fell back again in front of him.

'Cor, Mister, that's great!' said Joshua, wide-eyed.

Mr Bannerjee was as amazed himself. He felt more excited and energetic than he could ever remember.

He stood up. So, all around him, did Grandmas and Mums and other Dads. He kicked the ball again and it curved and swerved along the grass. A Grandma jumped at it and sent it spinning between two flower-beds.

'Goal!' she shouted.

Never had there been such a match! Goal-posts were made from walking-sticks. Old men and ladies straightened out creaking joints and took up their positions on the field. Little children dashed in between. There was shouting and calling and movement everywhere. The ball seemed alive as it twisted and rolled from foot to foot. The ice-cream man and the park keeper stood amazed.

Meanwhile, the rainbow rain kept falling, pitting the surface of the pond with tiny circles of reflecting light. The children, poking with sticks by the edge, in-between the empty sandwich bags and crumpled cans, stopped in amazement. Shafts of sunlight caught the scales of tiny golden fish. The brown minnows and sticklebacks had been transformed.

'Eee, someone's emptied a goldfish bowl in 'ere!' gasped a child.

Tom scooped up his fishing-net and tipped the contents into his jam jar.

'It's a monster!' he gasped. The tiny creature had three golden humps and a forked tail. It stared solemnly at Tom through the glass and he fed it with crumbs of vinegar crisps and wafer biscuits.

Tilly Witch rubbed her bony fingers together with satisfaction.

Shadows lengthened. Everyone, with flushed, happy faces, sat on the grass together. Ice-cream and sandwiches were shared around, names and addresses were exchanged.

There was laughter and chatter, and hands were shaken, and backs were slapped, as people, regretfully, made their way out of the park to go home for their suppers.

It was quiet again.

Tilly Witch smiled as she tucked her Spell Book in her shopping-bag. The magic was beginning to wear off now. She hadn't used the centipede's legs, of course, and they were good for strenghening spells; but even without them it had been a very good day.

Tom, on his way home, peered hard into his glass jar. The monster had disappeared – there were only a few surprised minnows swimming round a soggy crisp packet. He frowned, shrugged his shoulders and ran after his sister.

THE TOOTH-BALL
by Philippa Pearce

Once upon a time there was a boy called Timmy who was sad because he was too shy to make friends.

His grandmother knew this; and she invited him to visit her on her birthday. She wrote to him: 'We'll make a birthday cake. You can blow out the candles and cut the first slice of cake and have my birthday wish for yourself.'

'There!' said Timmy's mother. 'And you can go to Granny's by yourself, on the bus. You're old enough.'

And his father said: 'Don't forget to take your Granny a birthday present.'

So Timmy bought her a box of her favourite chocolates, each chocolate wrapped separately in gold foil.

At his grandmother's, they made the cake and iced it and stuck candles on top and lit them.

Timmy sang 'Happy birthday to you!' and then blew the candles out.

He began to cut the first slice of cake.

'Don't forget to wish,' said his grandmother.

'I don't believe in wishes,' Timmy said sadly.

'Then I'll wish something for you.'

'What?'

'That's secret. But something special.'

So she wished, as Timmy cut the cake, and they began eating.

Presently Timmy said: 'Here's half an almond.'

'We didn't put any almonds into the cake,' said his grandmother.

'It's not an almond,' said Timmy, examining it. 'It's a tooth. My tooth, that's been wobbling and wobbling. It's come out at last. Was that your special wish, Granny?'

But his grandmother wouldn't say. She remarked: 'You could put that tooth under your pillow tonight, Timmy, and by morning the fairies might have left some money in its place.'

'I don't believe in fairies,' said Timmy.

'Very likely,' said his grandmother. 'But take care of that tooth, anyway. You never know . . .'

And she gave Timmy the gold foil from one of her birthday chocolates to wrap his tooth in. 'Go on wrapping that tooth,' she said. 'Wrap it up well.'

Timmy went home with his gold tooth in his pocket.

He asked his mother for some silver kitchen-foil to wrap it in. So now it was wrapped in a layer of gold and a layer of silver on top of that.

The next day Timmy took out his silver tooth – rather a big tooth now – and wrapped it in a large green leaf from the garden. So now the tooth was wrapped in a layer of gold, a layer of silver, and a layer of green. By now it was much larger, and not really tooth-shaped any more, it was ball-shaped.

The next day Timmy wrapped his tooth-ball in some red paper left over from Christmas. So now the tooth was wrapped in layers of gold and silver and green and red.

The tooth-ball was getting bigger and bigger; but, oddly enough, it was not getting heavier.

Every day now Timmy added another layer of wrapping to his tooth-ball: a layer of writing-paper, of brown paper, of computer paper. By now the tooth-ball was bigger than a tennis-ball, but much, much lighter.

One day Timmy was playing in the front garden with his tooth-ball, when it sailed over the fence into the road. A boy who was passing caught it, and brought it back to Timmy.

'It's a strange ball,' said the boy.

'It's a tooth-ball,' said Timmy, and he explained all about it.

The boy said: 'My name's Jim, and I live in the next street. I've an old grey sock at home which would go over your tooth-ball, if you'd like that.'

'My name's Timmy,' said Timmy, 'and I would.'

So they went together to Jim's house and wrapped the tooth-ball in a layer of grey sock.

From now on Timmy and Jim together added a new wrapping to the tooth-ball every day.

They wrapped it in kitchen paper and newspaper and wallpaper. They wrapped it in cotton wool. They

wrapped it in a duster and a teatowel and an old woolly hat. They wrapped it in a tablecloth and a pillow-case and a sack.

It got bigger and bigger – and lighter and lighter, too, in a most surprising way. They had to wrap it in garden netting so that Timmy could wind his fingers in it firmly, to stop the tooth-ball from bouncing away.

Timmy and Jim took the tooth-ball to the park with them. They were playing with it, when a breeze blew it high over a clump of bushes and out of sight.

Timmy and Jim rushed round the bushes and came upon a whole gang of children who had been playing together. Now they were just standing and staring at the tooth-ball, which sat on the ground in the middle of them, looking interesting.

'Whatever is it?' asked a girl.

And a boy said, 'It's a huge raggedy balloon.'

'No,' said Timmy, 'It's a tooth-ball.' And he told them all the layers of wrapping; and Jim helped him to remember them in the right order.

Then they all began to play with the tooth-ball, batting it to and fro with their hands. By now the breeze had strengthened into a wind, which caught the tooth-ball and began to carry it up and away.

'Oh!' shrieked Timmy; and he caught the tooth-ball by a dangling end of netting as it was sailing past. But, instead of Timmy pulling the tooth-ball to earth, the tooth-ball lifted Timmy skyward.

'Hold on to him someone!' shouted Jim; and someone – a boy called Ginger – did. But the tooth-ball was carrying both of them upwards; so a girl caught hold of Ginger's ankles. Still they went up, all three of them. Then a boy caught the girl's feet, in the nick of time. Then a girl caught hold of him. Then another boy. Lastly, Jim.

The tooth-ball carried them all up and away, a trail of children in the sky.

They were blown on and on.

At last the wind died and they floated gently into a

back garden that Timmy knew well. His grandmother came out of the house to greet them: 'Timmy, how nice that you've dropped in! And all your friends, too! I'll get tea.'

When she came back with the lemonade and the chocolate biscuits and the crisps, she found Timmy and all the others staring dolefully at the tooth-ball.

'It's gone dead,' said Timmy. 'Heavy.'

'We must find out what's wrong,' said Timmy's grandmother. 'We'll have to unwrap it.'

They took off the netting and the sack and the pillow-case and the tablecloth and the woolly hat and the teatowel and the duster and the cotton wool and the wallpaper and the newspaper and the kitchen paper and the grey sock and the computer-paper and the brown paper and the writing-paper and the red paper and the green leaf and the silver foil – they took off all the layers of wrapping until, at the very centre of the ball, they came to the gold foil that Timmy had wrapped his tooth in, first of all.

But the gold foil was just a flat little bit of wrapping: there was no tooth inside it now.

'I was afraid of that,' said Timmy's grandmother. 'That tooth just wore itself out and *went*.'

'But a tooth doesn't do that,' said Timmy.

'A magic tooth does,' said his grandmother. 'This proves it.'

So, after tea, Timmy and his friends had to go home in the ordinary way, by bus.

Timmy was never able to make another tooth-ball; but he didn't mind too much. He had lots of friends instead.

And that's the end of the story.

THE OUTSIDE CAT
by Jane Thayer

Samuel was an outside cat.
He was an outside cat because he never was allowed inside.

The people in the house were good to Samuel.

They put bits of meat and sometimes a saucer of milk in the yard for him. They did not invite him in, because they had an inside cat.

On cold winter days, when even Samuel's fur coat could not keep him warm, he could see the inside cat sitting snugly at a window looking out.

He decided to be an inside cat if he could manage it.

Sometimes the inside cat came out for a breath of air and a stroll around the garden. Samuel explained that he would like to be an inside cat. The inside cat yawned.

'But you can't be an inside cat.'

'Why?' said Samuel.

'Because I'm the inside cat.' And the inside cat got up lazily and went to the door, which opened for him, but shut in Samuel's face.

In spite of what the inside cat said, Samuel still hoped to be an inside cat. He watched the door closely. He saw that when the postman came the front door always opened.

That was the way to get in!

The next time he saw the postman coming, he rushed to the front door and slipped inside.

But someone put him out before the door closed.

He saw that when the laundryman came the back door always opened.

That was the way to get in!

When he saw the laundryman coming, he rushed to the back door and slipped inside.

Someone put him out before the door closed.

Samuel saw a shelf outside the window, where the people put flowerpots in summer. He jumped on the shelf and looked in.

'If I can *see* in, why can't I *get* in? Miaow!' he said. 'Let me in!'

The inside cat jumped up inside the window. 'Miaow!' he said. 'Go away!'

So Samuel sat outside the door. He felt sure that if he sat there long enough he would get in.

People went in and came out. Samuel dodged inside between their legs. Everyone picked him up – politely, of course – and put him outside, saying, 'You are an outside cat.'

One day Samuel was sitting outside the door, waiting to get in, when he saw a big van stop in front of the house. Two men got out. They opened the back of the van. They came up the path and rang the bell. The door opened and they went in.

So did Samuel.

Nobody stopped him or put him out. At last I am in this house, thought Samuel, and I am going to stay!

I'll get under this chair and they won't know I'm here.

He was sitting quietly under the chair when, to his great surprise, somebody picked up the chair and carried it off.

Well, thought Samuel. I shall get under that table.

He was sitting under the table when, to his great surprise, somebody picked up the table and carried it off.

What's going on here? thought Samuel in alarm. I'd better get under that bed.

Somebody picked up the bed and carried that off, too.

And there sat Samuel in an empty house!

All the furniture had been moved out.

All the people had moved out.

Even the inside cat had moved out!

This is a fine thing, said Samuel to himself in disgust. He walked around the house. He couldn't find a bite of food or even a soft spot where he could take a nap. So finally he decided that he might as well go out. Only he didn't see any way to get out.

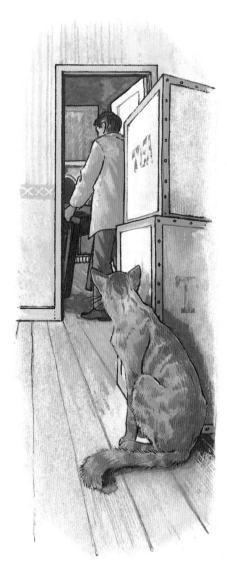

He jumped on the window sill, where he had often seen the inside cat sitting, and looked out.

'If I can *see* out,' he said, 'why can't I *get* out? Miaow!'

But he couldn't get out. He jumped down and went to the back door, but it was closed. He went to the front door, but it was closed. By this time Samuel was very anxious to be an outside cat once more.

He wandered about the house looking for a way out.

Suddenly Samuel's ears pricked up. He rushed to the front door, as a man opened it. Samuel dodged between his legs and slipped outside at last. Then he crawled under a bush to calm down.

Men began to unload furniture from a furniture van.

They took in a chair.

They took in a table.

They took in rugs and a kitchen stove and all sorts of furniture. Then they closed up the van and drove off.

Some new people drove up in a car and went into the house.

Samuel watched it all.

He watched the house for several days.

It began to look cheerful and homely.

Finally he decided again that he would be an inside cat if he could manage it. He marched boldly to the front door and sat down.

Someone opened the door and came out to cut a branch of red berries from a bush.

Samuel leaped up the steps.

'Here is somebody's cat,' said the people.

'Go home, kitty.'

Samuel went to the back door.

Someone opened the door and came out to get some wood from a pile.

This time he managed to slip inside.

No one saw him.

At last I am in this house, thought Samuel, and I am going to stay! I'll get under this chair and they won't know I'm here.

He got under the chair and fell asleep.

The people in the house put the red berries in a yellow bowl.

They put the logs in the fireplace and built a crackling fire.

They sat around the fire while the flames danced in the fireplace.

'How cosy it looks,' they said, 'with red berries in a yellow bowl and flames dancing in the fireplace! All we need is a pussycat curled up in front of our fire!'

At that moment Samuel woke up. He heard the fire crackling. He crawled out from under the chair.
He stretched and he yawned, and he sat down to blink at the fire just as if he were the inside cat and belonged there.

'Why, here's that cat!' cried the people.

They all looked at Samuel.

'Maybe he hasn't got any home,' they said. 'Let's let him stay and be our cat.'

Samuel pretended he wasn't listening, but his ears twitched.

'It's a smart outside cat who gets to be an inside cat!' he said to himself.

Then he curled up in front of the lovely fire, and purred!

JASON'S RAINBOW
by Joan Aiken

Jason walked home from school every day along the
side of a steep grassy valley, where harebells grew
and sheep nibbled. As he walked, he always whistled.
Jason could whistle more tunes than anybody else at
school, and he could remember every tune that he had
ever heard. That was because he had been born in a
windmill, just at the moment when the wind changed
from south to west. He could see the wind, as it blew; and
that is a thing not many people can do. He could see
patterns in the stars, too, and hear the sea muttering
charms as it crept up the beach.

One day, as Jason walked home along the grassy path,
he heard the west wind wailing and sighing. 'Oh, woe,
woe! Oh, bother and blow! I've forgotten how it goes!'

'What have you forgotten, Wind?' asked Jason, turning
to look at the wind. It was all brown and blue and
wavery, with splashes of gold.

'My tune! I've forgotten my favourite tune.'

'The one that goes like this?' said Jason, and he whistled.

51

The wind was delighted. 'That's it! That's the one! Clever Jason!' And it flipped about him, teasing but kindly, turning up his collar, ruffling his hair.

'*I'll give you a present*,' it sang to the tune Jason had whistled. '*What shall it be? A golden lock and a silver key?*'

Jason couldn't think what use *those* things would be, so he said quickly, 'Oh please, what I would like would be a rainbow of my very own to keep.' For in the grassy valley, there were often beautiful rainbows to be seen, but they never lasted long enough for Jason.

'A rainbow of your own? That's a hard one,' said the wind. 'A very hard one. You must take a pail and walk up over the moor till you come to Peacock Force. Catch a whole pailful of spray. That will take a long time. But when you have the pail full to the brim, you may find somebody in it who might be willing to give you a rainbow.'

Luckily the next day was Saturday. Jason took a pail, and his lunch, and walked over the moor to the waterfall that was called Peacock Force because the water, as it dashed over the cliff, made a cloud of spray in which wonderful peacock colours shone and glimmered.

All day Jason stood by the fall, getting soaked, catching the spray in his pail. At last, just at sunset, he had the whole pail filled up, right to the brim. And now, in the pail, he saw something that swam swiftly round and round – something that glimmered in brilliant rainbow colours.

It was a small fish.

'Who are you?' said Jason.

'I am the Genius of the waterfall. Put me back and I'll reward you with a gift.'

'Yes,' said Jason quickly, 'yes, I'll put you back, and please may I have a rainbow of my very own, to keep in my pocket?'

'Humph!' said the Genius. 'I'll give you a rainbow, but rainbows are not easy to keep. I'll be surprised if you can even carry it home. However, here you are.'

And it leapt out of Jason's pail, in a high soaring leap, back into its waterfall, and, as it did so, a rainbow poured out of the spray and into Jason's pail. 'Oh, how beautiful!' breathed Jason, and he took the rainbow, holding it in his two hands like a scarf, and gazed at its dazzling colours. Then he rolled it up carefully, and put it in his pocket.

He started walking home.

There was a wood on his way, and in a dark place among the trees he heard somebody crying pitifully. He went to see what was the matter and found a badger in a trap.

'Boy, dear boy,' groaned the badger, 'let me out, or men will come with dogs and kill me.'

'How can I let you out? I'd be glad to, but the trap needs a key.'

'Push in the end of that rainbow I see in your pocket; you'll be able to wedge open the trap.'

Sure enough, when Jason pushed the end of the rainbow between the jaws of the trap, they sprang open, and the badger was able to clamber out. 'Thanks, thanks,' he gasped, and then he was gone down his hole.

Jason rolled up the rainbow and put it back in his pocket; but a large piece had been torn off by the sharp teeth of the trap, and it blew away.

On the edge of the wood was a little house where old Mrs Widdows lived. She had a very sour nature. If children's balls bounced into her garden, she baked

them in her oven until they turned to coal. Everything she ate was black – burnt toast, black tea, black olives.

She called to Jason. 'Boy, will you give me a bit of that rainbow I see sticking out of your pocket? I'm very ill. The doctor says I need a rainbow pudding to make me better.'

Jason didn't much want to give Mrs Widdows a bit of his rainbow, but she did look ill, so, rather slowly, he went into her kitchen, where she cut off a large bit of the rainbow with a breadknife.

Then she made a stiff batter, with hot milk and flour, stirred in the piece of rainbow, and cooked it. She let it get cold and cut it into slices and ate them with butter and sugar. Jason had a small slice too. It was delicious.

'That's the best thing I've eaten for a year,' said Mrs Widdows. 'I'm tired of black bread. I can feel this pudding doing me good.'

She did look better. Her cheeks were pink and she almost smiled. As for Jason, after he had eaten his small slice of pudding, he grew three inches.

'You'd better not have any more,' said Mrs Widdows.

Jason put the last piece of rainbow in his pocket.

There wasn't a lot left now.

As he drew near the windmill where he lived, his sister Tilly ran out to meet him. She tripped over a rock and fell, gashing her leg. Blood poured out of it, and Tilly, who was only four, began to wail. 'Oh, my leg! It hurts dreadfully! Oh Jason, please bandage it, *please*!'

Well, what could he do? Jason pulled the rest of the rainbow from his pocket and wrapped it round Tilly's leg. There was just enough. He tore off a tiny scrap, which he kept in his hand.

Tilly was in rapture with the rainbow round her leg. 'Oh! how beautiful! And it has stopped the bleeding!' She danced away to show everybody.

Jason was left looking rather glumly at the tiny shred of rainbow between his thumb and finger. He heard a whisper in his ear and turned to see the west wind frolicking, all yellow and brown and rose-coloured.

'Well?' said the west wind. 'The Genius of the waterfall did warn you that rainbows are hard to keep! And, even *without* a rainbow, you are a very lucky boy. You can see the pattern of the stars, and hear my song, and you have grown three inches in one day.'

'That's true,' said Jason.

'Hold out your hand,' said the wind.

Jason held out his hand, with the piece of rainbow in it, and the wind blew, as you blow on a fire to make it burn bright. As it blew, the piece of rainbow grew and grew, until it lifted up, arching into the topmost corner of the sky; not just a single rainbow, but a double one, with a second rainbow underneath *that*, the biggest and most brilliant that Jason had ever beheld. Many birds were so astonished at the sight that they stopped flying and fell, or collided with each other in mid air.

Then the rainbow melted and was gone.

'Never mind!' said the west wind. 'There will be another rainbow tomorrow; or if not tomorrow, next week.'

'And I *did* have it in my pocket,' said Jason.

Then he went in for his tea.

THE ARGUING BOY
By Leila Berg

Now this is a tale of a boy who argued. And this is the way *I* tell it.

Once upon a time there was a boy. And he had nine big sisters. And because there were nine of them and only one of him, he always argued.

One day he had argued so much with his nine big sisters that he decided to seek his fortune. His mammy made him sandwiches – jam butties, he called them – and she put them in a bag, and he tied them to a pole over his shoulder, which is what people do when they seek their fortune, and off he went.

The weather was terrible. It poured. The rain went straight down his collar, shot down his back, and came out of the bottom of his jeans. And his sandwiches turned into pudding. He walked along, squelch, squelch.

At last he came to a house. He decided to knock at the door and ask if he could sleep there, in the dry.

'Can I sleep in your house?' he said to the lady.

'I'm afraid you can't.'

'But I'm sopping wet,' he said, starting to argue.

'I know you are, you poor wee thing,' she said. 'But I haven't got room.'

'You've got plenty of room,' he said arguing. 'You've got a whole house.'

'I'm afraid it's full of people. Tell you what, I'll give you some hot soup to make you feel better. There's plenty of that still cooking.'

'I don't want hot soup. I want to sleep here.' He was very rude.

Just then, the lady's husband put his head out of the door. 'Having trouble?' he said. 'Trying to sell you a vacuum cleaner, is he?'

'He wants to sleep here,' said the lady. 'I've told him we haven't got room.'

'I should say we have *not*,' said the man. 'We've a big party here, and people are sleeping everywhere.'

'They can't be *everywhere*. There must be *some* room,' said the boy, arguing away, moving his feet on the doorstep, squelch, squelch.

'There's no room at all,' said the man. 'But I'll tell you what –' and here he started to whisper in the woman's ear.

'Oooh!' said the woman. 'He couldn't!'

'Yes I can!' said the boy. He was just arguing.

Whisper, whisper, went the man. 'Oooh! he'd be scared to death!' said the woman.

'I wouldn't!' said the boy, arguing again.

Whisper, whisper, went the man. And this time the woman said, 'Well, you can tell him. But don't blame me if the Bogey gets him.'

Then the man said to the boy, 'You see, it's like this. We've got a cottage next door. There's nobody in it because of the little Red Bogey.'

'The little Red Bogey? What's that?'

'Oh, he's a sort of hobgoblin. Very fierce and bad-tempered. Perhaps you'd better not go in.'

'I will,' said the boy.

'I thought you would,' said the man. And he gave him the key.

Inside the cottage it was dry, but very dusty. No one had cleaned there for years, because of the little Red Bogey.

The boy found a pile of firewood and lit a fire with some matches he found on a shelf. Soon it was blazing away. He took off his boots, spread his clothes on the floor to dry off, and lay down on the bed in the corner.

He was almost asleep in the flickering firelight and the steam was coming up from his clothes and boots, when a voice said, 'I am coming!'

He didn't take much notice. After a moment, the voice said again, rather louder, 'I AM COMING!' He still took no notice.

But after another moment the voice fairly bawled, **'I AM COMING!'**

He sat up and shouted, 'If you are coming then COME, or else shut up!'

A pile of soot fell down from the chimney. Then two

dead birds who had been stuck there goodness knows how long. Then a lumpy red foot reached down, then a second one, then the rest of the two lumpy legs, then a lumpy, bumpy, frumpy-looking little red man came scrabbling down the bricks, and jumped right across the fire into the room.

'Well, what a shrimp!' said the boy. 'The noise you were making, I thought you were a giant at least!'

'Don't you talk to me like that!' said the little man. 'I'm the Red Bogey.'

'I don't care if you're a pink cauliflower,' said the boy.

The little man strode to the door and flung it open. Two men were standing there, one on each side, and they really *were* giants. 'We've got trouble here,' he said. 'Arguing boy. I may be needing you.'

The first one saluted. 'Just give us a call, Sir.'

'We'll chop him in pieces,' said the second.

'Right,' said the little Red Bogey. 'Stay there.' And he closed the door again.

'Now are you frightened?' he said to the boy.

'Not a bit,' said the boy.

The little Red Bogey scowled at him, then strode into the kitchen. 'Follow me!' he shouted.

'Why should I?' said the boy.

'You'll be sorry if you don't,' said the little Red Bogey.

'Who says so?' said the boy.

'You'll be sorry if you don't,' said the little Red Bogey, grinding his teeth and swishing his tail, 'because I am going to show you something very interesting indeed, and you will be very sorry if you miss it.'

The boy thought a minute or two, then followed him. 'I *might* come,' he said.

The little Red Bogey pulled open a trap door in the kitchen floor. Underneath were stairs leading to the cellar. 'Get down there!' he said.

'Why should I?' said the boy.

'You're frightened of the dark, I bet,' said the little Red Bogey.

'I am *not!*' said the boy. And he went down.

At the bottom was an enormous chest. 'Open it!' said the little Red Bogey.

'Open it yourself!' said the boy.

'Oh, you really are a nuisance,' said the little Red Bogey. 'You really make me so tired.' And he started to pull at the lid. He was very small, and the chest was very big, and the lid very heavy by the look of it. But the boy didn't help him at all.

The little Red Bogey kicked the chest, and pulled it, and shouted at the boy. 'You're as bad as I am!'

In the end, after a particularly heavy thump, the lid flew open and there was a pile of golden coins inside, flashing and glittering.

'Here! Who does that belong to?' said the boy.

'It's mine. All mine,' said the little Red Bogey.

'I don't believe you,' said the boy.

'Yes it is!' shouted the little Red Bogey. 'But I'm giving it to you, if you'll only give me a chance. I'm giving it to you and the people next door.'

'No, you're not,' said the boy. 'Where did you get it?'

'I stole it.'

'Then give it back.'

'I can't give it back. It was hundreds of years ago. I've been trying to give it away over and over again, but everyone runs away from me.'

'Well, it's nothing to do with me. I don't want it,' said the boy, and started to go up the steps again.

'It's a rule!' shouted the little Red Bogey. 'I stole it from a human being. So I've got to give it back to a human being. That's the rule!'

The boy stood still and thought, while the little Red Bogey waved his tail like an angry cat.

Then he said, 'Oh well, if there's a rule, that's different. All right, I'll take it.'

'Thank goodness for that,' said the little Red Bogey. 'Let me get away from you and have some peace.' And he dashed up the steps, and the boy came into the room just in time to see his red knobbly feet vanishing up the chimney.

'I wonder if the giants are still outside the door,' he said. But they'd gone too.

In the morning, the man and the woman from next door came round to see if he was all right. They were pleased to find him still there, and very surprised to hear about the money. Very pleased too.

The boy bought four tins of paint with some of his share, and painted the cottage yellow and white so that he could live there. Later he asked their daughter to marry him, and when she said no, he argued.

But she said, 'If you argue with me, I'll never speak to you again. Ask me again next year, without arguing in-between.'

And the next year she said yes.

They had twelve children, six of them boys, six of them girls. And none of them ever argued, not even about how that chestful of money had got into the cottage in the first place.

Snip snap snover
That story's over